A Spy

Jessica held up the map so they could all see it. There was some writing on it in beautiful, fancy script.

"What does it say?" Eva asked.

Jessica began to read out loud. "Listen! Hark! In the dark, find this mark, then embark!"

"That must be the code that Karl couldn't understand," Elizabeth said.

The sound of running feet made them spin around.

"The other elf!" Jessica yelled.

"Fritzi," Elizabeth added.

The Snoopers were all thinking the same thing. Fritzi was trying to get Santa's magic bell, too, but he might not have good intentions.

"Did he see the map?" Winston asked.

"I think he did," Elizabeth said with a shiver. "There's no time to lose."

SWEET VALLEY KIDS
SUPER SNOOPER #2

THE CASE OF THE MAGIC CHRISTMAS BELL

Written by
Molly Mia Stewart

Created by
FRANCINE PASCAL

Illustrated by
Ying-Hwa Hu

A BANTAM SKYLARK BOOK®
NEW YORK · TORONTO · LONDON · SYDNEY · AUCKLAND

RL 2, 005–008

THE CASE OF THE MAGIC CHRISTMAS BELL
A Bantam Skylark Book / December 1991

*Sweet Valley High® and Sweet Valley Kids are
trademarks of Francine Pascal*

Conceived by Francine Pascal

*Produced by Daniel Weiss Associates, Inc.
33 West 17th Street
New York, NY 10011*

Cover art by Susan Tang

*Skylark Books is a registered trademark of Bantam Books, a
division of Bantam Doubleday Dell Publishing Group, Inc.
Registered in U.S. Patent and Trademark Office and elsewhere.*

ISBN 0-553-15964-X

Published simultaneously in the United States and Canada

*Bantam Books are published by Bantam Books, a division of
Bantam Doubleday Dell Publishing Group, Inc. Its trademark,
consisting of the words "Bantam Books" and the portrayal of a
rooster, is Registered in U.S. Patent and Trademark Office and in
other countries. Marca Registrada. Bantam Books, 666 Fifth
Avenue, New York, New York 10103.*

PRINTED IN THE UNITED STATES OF AMERICA
CWO   0 9 8 7 6 5 4 3 2 1

To Emily Taryn Arlook

CHAPTER 1

A Special Present

Jessica Wakefield tiptoed into the living room at bedtime and stared at the Christmas tree. Christmas was only three days away, and there were plenty of presents piled under the twinkling lights of the tree.

She looked carefully over her shoulder. No one was in sight. She knelt down and began to examine the packages.

"What are you doing?" came a surprised voice behind her.

Jessica dropped the red-and-green wrapped gift she was holding. "Hi, Liz," she said, looking guilty.

Jessica's twin sister, Elizabeth, walked into the living room. She shook her head. "Jessica, you're such a snoop!"

"I know," Jessica admitted. "I can't help it."

Jessica loved secrets and mysteries. She and Elizabeth and some of their friends had started a detective club called the Snoopers. The biggest mystery of all, though, was how Jessica and Elizabeth could be identical twins, and still be so different from one another.

The two girls looked almost exactly alike. They both had blue-green eyes and long blond hair with bangs. When they wore identical outfits to school, the only way to tell them apart was by looking at their name bracelets.

The twins may have looked the same on the outside, but their personalities were very different. Elizabeth loved school and playing all

2

kinds of sports. Jessica loved dolls and hated getting her clothes messy. The twins even had different favorite colors. Jessica's was pink, and Elizabeth's was green. But even though they were different in so many ways, Jessica and Elizabeth were best friends.

"Don't try to guess what the presents are," Elizabeth said. "You'll ruin the surprise."

"I just want to see who they're from," Jessica said, picking up a gift. "This one's for me, from Great-Aunt Helen!"

Great-Aunt Helen was their mother's aunt, and she was one of the twins' favorite relatives. They never knew what fun and unusual ideas Great-Aunt Helen had up her sleeve.

Jessica began squeezing the gift through the wrapping paper. "It's hard and lumpy," she said. "Maybe it's a doll."

Just then, the twins' older brother, Steven,

3

walked into the room. "Hey!" he said. "You're not supposed to peek!"

"I'm not peeking," Jessica told him. She hid the gift she was holding behind her back.

"Put it down," Steven said. He tried to grab it from her.

"Quit it!" Jessica screamed.

They both hung onto the present and tugged on it. Suddenly, there was a ripping sound, and the paper tore away. A ten-inch-high, carved wooden elf fell onto the floor.

"Uh-oh," said Elizabeth.

Jessica bent over. The elf's left arm was cracked. "You broke my present!" she wailed.

"I didn't do it on purpose," Steven said. "Anyway, you'll still be able to play with it." He shrugged his shoulders and headed upstairs.

Elizabeth picked up the elf and tried to wrap

it back up, but the elf's red cap and green clothes still showed through the torn paper. "It's a really nice present," she said, trying to cheer up her sister. She put the elf back under the tree.

Jessica didn't answer. She looked very sad.

"Let's go to bed," Elizabeth said quietly.

Jessica nodded. All she had wanted was to try to guess what the present was. Now the surprise was spoiled, and so was the present. She went up the stairs slowly, dragging her feet.

"Sleep well, little elf," she whispered, as she climbed into bed. Then she turned over and went to sleep.

A noise from downstairs woke Jessica up. When she opened her eyes, faint daylight showed under the blinds. "Lizzie, are you awake?" she asked.

5

Elizabeth rolled over. "What is it?" she asked sleepily.

"I heard a noise," Jessica explained in a whisper. "Will you come downstairs with me?"

"OK," Elizabeth said, sitting up in bed.

The twins crept down the stairs. Strange sounds were coming from the kitchen. Jessica could feel her heart pounding inside her chest. The twins stopped in front of the kitchen door and looked nervously at each other.

"I'll open the door," Elizabeth said bravely. "One, two, three!"

When the door swung open, the girls saw an astonishing sight. A little person in green knickers, a green vest, and a red peaked cap was trying to climb onto the counter. He was no more than three feet tall, though, and couldn't quite make it.

"Who are you?" Jessica asked, her eyes wide.

The stranger turned around. "Oh, hi there. My name is Karl. I was trying to find something to eat," he explained. "But my arm hurts."

Jessica's eyes opened even wider. She gulped and stared at Elizabeth. "It's my elf!" she exclaimed. "He's gotten taller and come to life!"

"Of course I'm alive," Karl said proudly. "Santa chose me for an important mission. Tell me, is this what they call TV?" He switched on the portable television set on the counter. Speechless, the twins looked at the elf. He sat down in a chair, dangled his legs over the edge, and smiled at the TV.

"What mission are you talking about?" Jessica asked at last.

Karl jumped down from the chair and stood looking up at the twins. "Every Christmas Eve, Santa lets the reindeer stop somewhere to

7

rest and have a snack. Last year, the magic jingle bell that gives the reindeer the power to fly fell off of Donner's harness while they were stopped. There was enough magic left to finish up and get back to the North Pole, but this year . . ." He shrugged.

Jessica looked worried. "You mean, Santa won't be able to come at all this year unless you find that bell?" she asked.

"Right." Karl took a folded piece of paper from his pocket. "Santa didn't even realize the magic bell was missing until he started polishing up the sleigh yesterday. He gave me a map so I could find the place where they stopped last year. There's just one little problem. Santa makes his maps in code, in case they should fall into the wrong hands. And I can't figure this one out!"

9

CHAPTER 2

The Christmas Parade

Elizabeth tugged on Jessica's arm. "Psst," she said. "Come out in the hall for a minute."

While Karl returned to watching television, the twins left the kitchen. "Don't you think this is weird?" Elizabeth asked. "Maybe we should wake up Mom and Dad."

"No!" Jessica said quickly. "You know how grown-ups are. They'll never believe he's a real elf."

"But, Jess! Karl *is* real!" Elizabeth said.

Jessica nodded. "I know, but—"

At that moment, they heard the back door close. Elizabeth and Jessica dashed into the kitchen. Karl was gone.

"Oh, no," Jessica said. "He's too little to go wandering off by himself. And his arm is hurt!"

Elizabeth nodded. "We have to find him," she said. "Let's look in the garden."

They ran out the back door and searched everywhere outside the house. There was no sign of Karl. In the distance, they could hear the sounds of marching bands tuning up for the Christmas parade.

"How is he ever going to find that magic bell?" Jessica asked, shaking her head. "He doesn't even understand the map."

"We have to help him," Elizabeth said.

"We have to find him first," Jessica reminded her.

They stared hopelessly down the empty

street. "I think we need some help," Elizabeth said. "Let's call a meeting of the Snoopers."

When Elizabeth and Jessica arrived at the parade a short while later, the other Snoopers were already there waiting for them.

"What's the big mystery?" Lila Fowler asked. The members of the Snoopers Club were always looking for a mystery to solve.

"Yeah," Todd Wilkins said. "Why couldn't you tell us over the phone?"

Eva Simpson, Amy Sutton, Ellen Riteman, and Winston Egbert were there, too. They were all eager to hear the twins' big secret. Suddenly, Elizabeth felt uncertain. How could they explain that Jessica's toy elf had come to life and needed their help to save Christmas?

"This is going to sound pretty strange,"

13

Jessica began. She nudged Elizabeth with one elbow. "You tell them."

Elizabeth fiddled nervously with her name bracelet. "Well, see, there's this elf."

"Karl," Jessica said.

"He's alive, and he needs our help," Elizabeth explained.

Amy's eyes opened wide. Then she held one finger up to her ear and twirled it around in a circle. "Cuckoo."

"It's not cuckoo!" Jessica said, stamping her foot. "Santa lost the magic sleigh bell that makes the reindeer fly right here in Sweet Valley last Christmas, and if Karl can't find it, there won't be a Christmas this year!"

A brass band started playing "Santa Claus is Coming to Town." Elizabeth and the other Snoopers all turned to look. Elizabeth was getting very worried. They didn't have much time to find the bell.

"We have to find Karl," she told her friends. "He needs help figuring out the map that Santa gave him."

Winston tapped his foot in time to the drum beat. "You're not joking around, are you?" he asked.

"No," Jessica answered.

"You promise you're not making this whole thing up?" Eva asked.

"We promise," Elizabeth and Jessica said at the same time. They looked very serious.

"OK," Lila said, folding her arms. "I believe you think it's true, but how do you know Karl is really an elf? Maybe he's kidding you."

"If you met Karl, you would know he's not

kidding," Elizabeth said. "He doesn't seem like he could tell a lie."

The Snoopers were very quiet for a moment. Elizabeth and Jessica looked at their friends. Only a day ago, they had all been excited about Christmas. But now they all looked sad, because this year, Santa might not be coming to town at all.

Unless they could find Karl and the missing bell.

16

CHAPTER 3

Elf Magic

Jessica looked around at the crowd. The sidewalks were filled with parents and kids and teenagers. Everyone looked happy and cheerful. But even though Jessica usually loved parades, she was much too worried to enjoy this one.

Then a short figure in green clothes caught her eye. "Hey! There's Karl!" she said, darting between two women. Up ahead, she could see Karl's back, and his head with the red cap. She ran as fast as she could. The others followed. At last, Jessica caught up to the elf and grabbed his arm.

"I found you—oops, sorry, I forgot your arm was hurt," she said, letting him go when he stared at her in shock.

"What are you talking about?" he said grumpily. He scowled at her and walked away briskly.

"What happened?" Elizabeth asked, running up with the other Snoopers.

Todd tried to find the elf in the crowd. "Why did you let him go?"

"I don't think that was Karl," Jessica said in a puzzled voice. "It didn't seem like him at all."

"Oh, so now you think there are *two* elves around here?" Lila asked doubtfully.

Elizabeth was looking in the opposite direction. "Is that him over there?" she asked.

"He went the other way," Jessica explained, but she turned and looked where her sister was pointing. A large, decorated float was coming

18

down the street. It had pretend reindeer on wheels in front, and a man dressed as Santa Claus was riding on it. He was waving at the crowd, stopping now and then to hold his belly as he let out a jolly laugh. Karl, if it *was* Karl, was running toward the float.

"That's him!" Elizabeth said.

"He's going to try to talk to Santa Claus!" Ellen shouted.

Winston shook his head. "If other people find out he's a real elf . . ."

"We have to stop him," Amy said.

They all started to run, but the crowd was so packed that they could hardly go three steps without having to stop. Other kids glared at the Snoopers as they pushed their way to the front. Jessica could see Karl through the crowd. He was trying to climb up onto the Santa Claus float.

19

"Hurry!" Jessica said, as she squeezed past a double stroller.

A gap opened up in the crowd. The Snoopers burst through to the edge of the street, but a police officer held up his hands. "Whoa!" he said. "Slow down."

The Snoopers were trapped. They could only try to hear what Karl was telling the people on the float.

"Who do you think you are?" Karl scolded the pretend Santa Claus in a piercing voice. "You're not Santa Claus!"

"Karl!" Jessica shouted.

The man dressed as Santa Claus was trying to smile at all the children, but he kept pointing with his thumb to the back of the float. Jessica realized that he thought Karl was one of his helpers.

"I will not go back with those fake elves!"

Karl said, grabbing hold of the reins of the fake reindeer. The harness bells let out a loud jingle. "Give me those bells!"

"Who is that little fellow?" a policeman asked people in the crowd when he noticed what was happening.

The Snoopers couldn't get any closer to the float, because the police officer was still blocking their way. "Karl!" Jessica shouted again, as the sleigh moved slowly down the street. "Come with us! I'm sure the bell's not there!"

Karl was creating quite a commotion. Many of the people in the crowd were talking about him and wondering what he was doing. A reporter from the television station walked closer with her video camera.

"Karl!" Jessica and Todd and Winston shouted together.

At that moment, Karl raised his hands over

his head and clapped them three times. All the bells on the harness suddenly popped off and hung in the air all by themselves.

The sleigh stopped. The music stopped. Everyone stood and stared at the bells. There wasn't a sound except for the jingle bells ringing.

Then the crowd went wild.

"Did you see that?"

"That was magic!"

"How did that little guy do that?"

"What's going on here?"

"Somebody grab that ELF!"

CHAPTER 4

The Bad Elf

Elizabeth listened to the shouting and yelling all around her. If everyone made a big fuss over Karl, he wouldn't be able to carry out his mission. She knew that he needed the Snoopers more than ever now.

"Come on, let's get him out of here," Lila said in a low voice.

But before they could get to Karl, he was surrounded by police officers, reporters, and curious bystanders. "We'd like to ask you a few questions," one of the police officers began.

Karl stared up at them in surprise. Then he ducked between their legs and dashed away.

"Follow him!" called out a high, piercing voice. "He went that way!"

Elizabeth turned to see who had spoken. It was another elf—the one Jessica had seen before.

"He's hiding under that car!" the second elf screamed.

"Who are you?" Elizabeth asked him angrily. "Why are you trying to get Karl in trouble?"

The elf stuck out his tongue at her and ran after the police officers. Elizabeth and the other Snoopers could see someone reaching under a car. Then they heard Karl's voice, sounding muffled and upset.

"I'll tell Santa! You don't understand!" he said.

"Excuse me," Elizabeth said, trying to squeeze closer to the car.

"Get him!" the second elf yelled.

Karl was pulled, kicking and struggling, from under the car. He looked up at the other elf. "Fritzi! Help me!"

Fritzi just laughed and disappeared into the crowd.

Karl stopped struggling and stood still. A police officer was holding him by the arm. He looked confused.

"Karl? Are you OK?" Jessica asked, trying to get close to him.

Karl dug his free hand into his pocket. "Take this!" he begged, handing Jessica his folded map. "You have to find the bell. Christmas depends on you now!"

"What's that?" the police officer said.

Jessica backed away without answering. "Come on!" she yelled to the others. Elizabeth chased after her sister, with the rest of the Snoopers right behind her.

"Over here," Todd said, waving them all around the corner of a building.

"Whew," Ellen said. She stopped and bent over with her hands on her knees. "That was close!"

"Karl gave me the map," Jessica said as she unfolded it.

Winston looked back over his shoulder. "Did you see what he did with those bells? It was awesome!"

"Now do you believe he's a real elf?" Elizabeth asked.

"Sure," Winston said, nodding.

Lila crossed her arms. "If Karl can do magic, then why couldn't he get away from those people?"

"I don't know," Elizabeth admitted. "Maybe he only has a little bit of magic power."

Jessica held up the map against the wall of

the building so that they could all see it. There were lines and shapes on it, along with some writing in beautiful, fancy script.

"What does it say?" Eva asked.

"It's a poem, I think," Jessica said. She began to read out loud. "Listen! Hark! In the dark, find this mark, then embark."

The Snoopers all looked puzzled. "What's that supposed to mean?" Amy asked.

"That must be the code that Karl couldn't understand," Elizabeth said. "I don't get it, either."

The sound of running feet made them spin around just in time to see Fritzi disappear around the corner.

"The other elf!" Jessica said with a gasp.

"Fritzi," Elizabeth added.

"I think he's a bad elf," Ellen said nervously. "He *wanted* the police to catch Karl."

30

A worried silence fell on the group. They were all thinking the same thing. Fritzi was trying to get the bell, too, but he might not have good intentions.

"Did he see the map?" Winston asked.

"I think he did," Elizabeth said with a shiver. "There's no time to lose."

CHAPTER 5

Santa's Map

Jessica frowned as she carefully folded the map. She knew that it was her duty to help Karl. After all, he was her elf, and he had given her the map. She just hoped she'd be able to find the bell.

"That Fritzi sure is sneaky," Todd said.

"He's probably trying to spoil Christmas," Ellen said, beginning to sniffle. "That's not only sneaky, it's downright mean!"

"I agree," Eva said. "Maybe we should try to find out for sure what Fritzi is up to."

"Let's see if we can find Karl," Elizabeth suggested. "Maybe he'll know."

Jessica nodded. She wanted to make sure that Karl was all right, anyway. She hoped his arm didn't hurt too much.

The Snoopers headed back to the parade and soon spotted the police officers who had stopped Karl. The officers were standing to one side of a police car, deep in conversation. Inside the car, Jessica caught a glimpse of a red hat. "He's in the car," she whispered.

While the officers were looking in the opposite direction, the Snoopers crept silently to the other side of the car. They ducked out of sight.

"Pssst!" hissed Elizabeth.

The top of the red hat bobbed up and down as Karl looked out the window. "Hi!" he whispered. He seemed happy to see the twins.

"Shhh!" Jessica put one finger to her lips.

"We're going to figure out the map for you and find the bell."

"These are our friends," Elizabeth went on. She pointed to each of them. "Todd, Lila, Winston, Ellen, Eva, and Amy."

"How do you do?" Karl asked them. "I hope you can help me."

Jessica couldn't help smiling at him, even though she knew they had serious business to discuss.

"What can you tell us about that elf named Fritzi?" Todd asked Karl. "Can we trust him?"

"Fritzi?" Karl looked uncertain. "Well, Fritzi has always been a bit of a troublemaker. He's my cousin."

"Your cousin?" Elizabeth said. "Then why isn't he helping you?"

"He's jealous. He thinks Santa likes me better than him."

"Then he's out to make trouble," Lila said.

Karl scratched his head. "Well, Fritzi has said some mean things about Santa. He was telling everyone in the workshop that Santa's too old for the job. But I believe, deep down, that he's basically a good elf."

"Then why did he tell the police where you were hiding?" Amy asked.

Karl looked sad. "I don't know."

"Fritzi got a peek at the map," Winston said. "Do you think he's trying to find the bell, too?"

Before Karl could answer, the police officers looked back toward the car.

"We'd better get out of here," Elizabeth whispered.

Bending over, the Snoopers ran behind another car to hide.

"What do you think they're going to do with Karl?" Jessica asked, sounding worried.

"Let's see if we can hear where they're taking him," Todd suggested. He and Elizabeth crawled on their hands and knees as close to the squad car as they could get without being seen. After a moment, they hurried back.

"They're taking him to the TV station!" Elizabeth said excitedly.

"The news reporter talked them into it," Todd said. "She wants to interview Karl."

"But that could take a long time," Amy said. "My mom works at the TV station, and she told me all about what they do when they're filming an interview. It's really complicated."

Elizabeth looked at the others. "We'll just have to find the bell and take it to him there. I bet once he has it, he'll be able to escape with the magic of the bell."

"Until we find it, poor Karl will be stuck," Jessica said.

She raised her head to peek at what was going on. Just a few yards away, Fritzi was talking to a reporter. He saw her and gasped. Then he ran off into the crowd.

CHAPTER 6

Cooperation

"Come on!" Todd said, sprinting after Fritzi. The other Snoopers followed, but Fritzi had a head start. He disappeared into the crowd.

"It's no use," Winston said. He stopped and shook his head. "We'll never find him."

"Well, maybe we shouldn't waste any more time trying to find *him*," Lila said. "We're supposed to be trying to find the bell."

Elizabeth nodded. "Let's take another look at the map. Maybe there are more clues on it."

Jessica took the map out of her pocket. The

Snoopers put their heads together and studied it carefully. In one corner was another short poem. Elizabeth read it out loud. "Watery geography, perfect for a honeybee, this is public property, a canopy for feathery luxury."

Amy's mouth opened and closed. "What?" she finally said.

"It's some kind of riddle," Winston explained.

"Oh, that's really smart, Win," Lila said with a giggle. "Can you tell us what it means?"

Elizabeth closed her eyes and concentrated. "Everyone think! Christmas depends on us."

"That's right," Jessica said. "We're supposed to be detectives. This is a clue. We can figure it out."

"What about the pet store?" Eva said. "They have tons of birds there. That would be feathery."

"Pet stores don't have chimneys," Ellen pointed out. "I doubt Santa would stop there."

Jessica was thinking hard. "Karl said it's a place where the reindeer stopped to rest. Where would reindeer like to go?"

"I know!" Elizabeth shouted. "The zoo! It's public property."

"And it has ponds full of water," Todd went on eagerly. "And birds."

"And flowers for honeybees," Amy said.

Jessica jumped up and down in excitement. "They must have stopped at the zoo. There's lots of food there for reindeer!"

"Let's get over to the zoo," Elizabeth said. "And quick."

A half hour later, the Snoopers were each using their pocket money to buy tickets to the zoo. Eva's mother had agreed to drive them over in the Simpson family van, even though none of the kids could explain why they suddenly had to go to the zoo!

"Where should we go first?" Winston asked. He looked at the signs that read "Monkey House," "World of Birds," and "Camel Ride." "The bell could be in a lot of places."

"This way," Elizabeth said as she led them down a path. She wasn't sure they were even going in the right direction, but she figured they had to start looking somewhere.

A short way down the path, they came to the camel ride. There were dozens of children lined up to ride the camel, who was dressed up for Christmas in a special silver harness. The jingling of bells rang out with each step he took.

"Look!" Lila whispered, pointing to the fence.

A small person dressed in green and red was watching the camel.

"Fritzi!" they all said at once.

"This proves he *did* see the map!" Elizabeth said angrily.

"He doesn't know we're here, yet," Jessica said. "Let's sneak up behind him."

Very slowly and cautiously, the Snoopers spread out and surrounded Fritzi. Elizabeth was sure that this was their chance to find out once and for all what he was up to.

"Fritzi," she said.

Fritzi spun around. For a second, it looked like he was going to make a run for it. But when he saw that he was surrounded, he just smiled.

"Well, kids. I guess we had the same idea," he said cheerfully. "But I'm pretty sure none of the bells on the camel is the right one. They're too big."

"Are you telling the truth?" Elizabeth demanded.

Fritzi smiled innocently. "Of course! Listen, why don't you let me see the map up close. We're all in this together. I know Santa better than you do, so I can probably figure out his clues."

"How do we know you won't trick us?" Jessica asked.

"Trust me," Fritzi said.

Elizabeth didn't trust him one bit. But maybe he would be able to understand Santa's clues. After all, he *was* an elf.

"We don't have a lot of time," Fritzi reminded them. "If Santa doesn't have the bell by Christmas Eve, he won't be able to deliver any presents."

Elizabeth and Jessica looked at each other. "Todd, watch Fritzi while the rest of us have a private conference," Elizabeth said.

45

"I think he's lying," Winston whispered, as the Snoopers huddled together.

"Me, too," Eva said. "But maybe he can help us find the bell."

"If we all watch him like hawks, he won't be able to do anything tricky," Lila added.

"What do you think, Elizabeth?" Amy asked.

Elizabeth slowly shook her head. "Maybe we should keep him with us. At least that way we'll know he isn't sneaking off with the bell."

"That's true," Ellen agreed.

"I say we take him with us," Jessica said. "Who votes yes?"

One by one, the Snoopers all raised their hands.

CHAPTER 7

Fritzi's Story

The Snoopers had agreed to ride to the park on their bikes after lunch. They needed a private place to discuss the map and talk to Fritzi.

"I hope Todd and Winston haven't let Fritzi escape," Jessica said as she and Elizabeth pedaled down the sidewalk. The boys had taken Fritzi with them after Mrs. Simpson had dropped everyone off. "I still don't trust Fritzi. After all, he made sure Karl got caught."

"I know," Elizabeth said. She coasted a few feet. "But the only thing we can do for Karl is find the bell. And Fritzi might be the only one who can help us."

Jessica shook her head. She had a feeling that Fritzi was up to no good.

When the twins arrived at the park, they found the other Snoopers waiting by the swing set. Fritzi was sitting on a swing. His feet didn't even touch the ground.

"Listen, Fritzi," Jessica said, leaning her bike on its kickstand. "Before we let you see the map, you have to tell us why you're here."

"That's right," Lila said sternly. "What's your story?"

Fritzi kicked back with his legs and started swinging. He didn't seem to be very worried that Christmas was in danger.

"Are you and Karl friends?" Elizabeth asked.

"Oh, sure," Fritzi said with a big smile.

"He's my cousin. We work at Santa's toy shop together. Wherever Karl goes, I go."

Jessica frowned. *Friends don't turn friends over to the police*, she thought. But she kept silent.

"Karl is a great elf," Fritzi went on. "Santa even gave him a promotion this year, and nobody at the North Pole was prouder of Karl than I was."

"Does Santa like you?" Todd asked.

"Me?" Fritzi laughed. "Sure he does. He's a really great guy."

The Snoopers looked at each other silently. Fritzi's version of the story sounded very different from Karl's.

"Yessirree," Fritzi went on, swinging back and forth. "Santa's terrific, and so is Karl. I was really proud when he got promoted. We always worked together, but only one of us could get a promotion. So of course, Karl got it."

49

Jessica thought Fritzi was starting to sound a little jealous, just like Karl said he was. Maybe Fritzi wanted to get the bell to prove that he should have been promoted instead of Karl.

"You wouldn't try to spoil Christmas, would you?" asked Ellen.

Fritzi laughed again. "Me? Not a chance. But if I find the bell, I'll be making a few changes. Santa is a little too old-fashioned. If I had the bell, I'd be in charge."

"*You*'d be in charge?" Winston asked.

Fritzi jumped down off the swing and looked at them angrily. "That's right. And if you kids don't start cooperating, you won't get *any* presents when I take over Santa's job. Got it?"

"But—" Jessica began. She felt her stomach do a flip-flop. Fritzi would make a terrible replacement for Santa Claus!

51

"I'm not cooperating with you!" Eva said in a loud voice. She rarely lost her temper, but she looked very upset.

"Me, neither," Amy agreed.

Fritzi cocked his head to one side. "You'll never be able to find the bell by yourselves. And if you don't, that's the end of Christmas."

"We know that," Elizabeth said. She wasn't sure what to do next.

"But if you do cooperate with me, Christmas will still happen," Fritzi went on. He smiled crookedly. "So you don't have any choice!"

CHAPTER 8

Bells, Bells, Bells

Elizabeth had never felt so angry. "OK," she said, sighing and shaking her head. "Let's show Fritzi the map."

The others grumbled, but they agreed. Fritzi rubbed his hands together happily.

"I knew you were smart kids," he chuckled. "You won't be sorry."

Jessica glared at him as she took the map out of her pocket and opened it up. Fritzi pushed her out of the way to get a closer look.

"Hmm, yes," he mumbled. "Santa's old tricks again. Hmm, I wonder, no, maybe . . . Aha!"

Everyone looked at him hopefully. *Maybe showing Fritzi the map* was *the right thing to do*, thought Elizabeth.

"What is it?" Winston asked.

"See this line here?" Fritzi said. "And these wavy lines next to it? I'm pretty sure that means water."

"Watery geography!" Amy said, her eyes lighting up. "That's what the riddle says."

"Right, right," Fritzi muttered. "And this is a symbol for tree."

"Of course," Jessica said, snapping her fingers. "A canopy of feathery luxury! Birds like trees."

"OK," Fritzi said. "So where is there some water and trees in this dumb old town?"

Elizabeth sent him an angry look. But they were running out of time. They had to cooperate, even if Fritzi was being rude.

"There's the public swimming pool," Ellen volunteered. "That has palm trees all around it."

Fritzi waved one hand impatiently. "No, no. Santa doesn't let the reindeer drink swimming pool water. He says it's bad for them. I think he spoils those dumb reindeer. It's all Donner's fault for losing the bell, anyway. I'll fire Donner when I'm in charge."

Lila made a face at Fritzi behind his back. "There's a reflecting pool at the office building where my father works," she said.

"But no trees," Jessica reminded her.

Deep in thought, Elizabeth looked around the park. Across the duck pond, the community Christmas tree sparkled in the sunshine. It made a beautiful reflection in the water. She blinked in surprise.

"That's it!" she yelled, grabbing the map out

of Fritzi's hands. "Listen, hark!" she read. "In the dark, find this mark, then embark. It all rhymes with park!" she said excitedly.

"You mean the missing bell is here in the park?" But where?" Jessica asked. "What do the other clues mean?"

"Watery geogra*phy*, perfect for a honey*bee*, this is public proper*ty*, a canopy of feathery luxu*ry*!" Elizabeth continued. "It all rhymes with Christmas *tree*!"

Jessica clapped her hands. "Of course Santa would stop at a Christmas tree!"

In a flash, Fritzi started running for the tree.

"Don't let him get there first!" Jessica screamed.

The Snoopers raced after him. Luckily, he was shorter than they were, so it was easy to catch up to him.

56

"What's the big idea?" Todd asked when they all stopped at the tree.

Fritzi smiled innocently. "I just got excited."

Elizabeth knew he was lying. But now they had to find out if they were at the right place.

"Oh, no!" Amy said, pointing at the tree. "Look!"

The whole Christmas tree was decorated with jingle bells. Each breeze that swayed the branches made the tree ring.

"It had bells on it last year, too," Ellen said.

Elizabeth was thinking fast. "If Santa stopped here and the bell fell off, then it could have been picked up when all the bells were taken off the tree after Christmas."

"The bell must be here," Fritzi said, his eyes scanning the tree. "Nice grass, clean water.

Just the kind of place that old softy would choose to rest the reindeer."

The Snoopers were positive they were at the right spot, too. But which one was the magic bell?

CHAPTER 9

Jingle, Jingle, Jingle

Fritzi raised his hands over his head and clapped them three times. All the bells came jingling and jangling off the branches and bounced onto the grass.

"Wow!" Eva said, kneeling down. "You can do magic just like Karl."

"Now you can find Santa's bell," Jessica said, keeping a sharp eye on Fritzi.

For the first time, Fritzi looked embarrassed. "Well, I don't really know which one it is," he said. "Only Karl knows how to tell. I guess we have to take them to him."

"All of them?" Elizabeth asked, opening her eyes wide. "We'll have to bring them all back later."

Eva, Ellen, Todd, and Winston were busily picking up the bells. Lila had a little purse with her, and Amy had a pouch on her belt. The Snoopers put some of the bells in those bags.

"We need something else to carry them in," Elizabeth said. "There are so many."

"How about our bicycle baskets?" Eva said.

Just then, a park gardener started walking toward them. "What's going on here?" he asked suspiciously.

Everyone froze. Everyone but Fritzi, that is. He clapped his hands three times again. "You don't see anyone," he said under his breath, staring at the gardener. "There's nobody here."

The gardener turned and strolled away, whistling "Deck the Halls."

"Wow," Todd whispered.

For a moment, nobody spoke. Then they quickly finished gathering up the bells. "Now we need a plan for getting to Karl," Jessica said. "He's probably still at the TV station."

They all looked at Amy. Her mother worked at the TV station. "We could ask to watch the Christmas show they're doing this afternoon at the television studio," Amy suggested.

Fritzi jumped up in the air and clicked his heels together. "The perfect cover!" he said gleefully. "Let's go!"

"Don't you try anything sneaky," Jessica warned. "You have to stay where we can see you."

"No problem," Fritzi said with a sly smile.

* * *

Mrs. Sutton arranged for all the Snoopers to come watch the taping of the Christmas special. They all told their parents what fun they were going to have at the studio. What they didn't tell their parents was that they were on a rescue mission.

Jessica was very worried about Karl. He was so friendly and innocent that she was afraid he might give away too many of Santa's important secrets without meaning to. There was no telling what he might let slip!

"What's that jingling sound?" Mr. Wakefield asked as Jessica, Elizabeth, and Eva climbed out of the car at the station. The others were meeting them there.

"Oh, it's just some coins in my pocket,"

Jessica fibbed, crossing her fingers behind her back.

Mr. Wakefield chuckled. "You sure sound rich! Have fun at the taping. I'll pick you up in an hour. Do everything Mrs. Sutton says, and don't get in the way."

"We won't, Dad," Elizabeth promised.

The other Snoopers and Fritzi were waiting in the lobby. Luckily, the receptionist was not at her desk. The coast was clear. They didn't want anyone to ask what they were up to. Mrs. Sutton had gotten permission for them to be part of the audience watching the taping of the show, but they knew they weren't supposed to be wandering around the building.

"This way," Amy whispered.

Each of them carried a bag stuffed with jingle bells. With every step they took, a loud

66

ching ching ching sounded in the empty hallway.

"Shh!" Fritzi said, putting his finger to his lips.

"Where could Karl be?" Jessica whispered.

Chingle ching ching.

"Your bells are too loud!" Lila said to Ellen.

"I can't help it!" Ellen answered. "Besides, yours are even louder!"

Step by step, they tiptoed down the hallway.

Chingly chingly ching.

"Someone is going to hear us!" Winston said.

"Where could Karl be?" Jessica asked again. She was worried that if they didn't find Karl soon, the whole TV station was going to hear them and ask what they were doing.

Ching ching CHING!

CHAPTER 10

The Magic Bell

The hallways of the TV station were very quiet. Elizabeth thought it seemed almost eerie. Up ahead, a large picture window showed a glimpse of lights and television cameras.

"What's that?" she whispered to Amy, pointing to the window.

"That's what they call a viewing window. You can see the studio from there," Amy explained.

"Do you think Karl might be in the studio?" Jessica asked.

"Maybe," Amy said.

Trying to keep the bells quiet, they all tip-toed to the window. From where they stood, they had a good view of the television cameras on wheels, the floodlights hanging from the ceiling, the microphone cords, and the people inside the studio.

The lights were all shining on a stage. Seven small children were sitting on the stage, while a woman asked them questions. A bright Christmas tree sparkled behind them.

"What's going on?" Todd asked.

"They're videotaping the Christmas special," Amy explained. "Those children are all patients from the Sweet Valley Hospital."

Elizabeth could see that the children all looked tired and pale. Two of them were in wheelchairs. She felt sad looking at them.

70

"Some Christmas special," Fritzi said. "It doesn't look very happy."

"Pssst!" Todd was farther down the hall, looking through a small glass panel. He waved at them. "I found Karl! He's behind this door."

Elizabeth and the other Snoopers hurried away from the viewing window. The bells they were carrying jingled noisily. When they reached the door, Todd turned the key that was in the doorknob. Karl was inside, sitting alone at a desk.

"Karl!" Jessica cried, running in and hugging him.

"Hi," he said. He smiled, but he looked lonely and sad.

Elizabeth knew exactly what to say to cheer him up. "We think we found the bell!" she told him.

"You did? That's great! I knew I could count on you," Karl said. He looked happier already.

"*I* did all the work," Fritzi snapped.

Elizabeth shook her head but didn't say anything. She didn't want Karl to know about all the mean things his cousin had said. She started taking jingle bells out of her pockets. The others did the same.

Soon there were jingle bells on the table, jingle bells on the chairs, and jingle bells rolling across the floor.

"Which bell is it?" Fritzi asked, watching as Karl picked one up.

"I can't tell by looking at them," Karl said. "I'll have to ring each one." He shook the bell he was holding. "That's not it."

"How about this one?" Jessica asked, ringing another.

"No, that's not it either." Karl climbed onto the table, ringing bell after bell.

Ellen and Lila stood by the door as look-outs. "Hurry," Lila said, peeking out the door. "Someone might come."

Each time Karl rang a bell, Jessica and Elizabeth put it back in a bag. Fritzi was pacing impatiently. The others watched and waited.

Jingle chingle.

"That's not it," Karl said.

Ringle dingle.

"That's not it," Karl said again.

Elizabeth felt excited, nervous, and hopeful all at once. *The magic bell has to be there*, she thought. *It just has to be.* There wasn't much time left.

Suddenly, a different sound filled the room. *Tingle-tingle-tingle!*

The silvery, chiming sound gave Elizabeth goose bumps. "Is that it?" she asked in a hushed voice.

Karl was smiling from ear to ear. "This is it!"

"Aha!" Fritzi jumped up onto the table and snatched the bell from Karl. "I'm in charge of Christmas, now!"

Before anyone could move, Fritzi barged past the look-outs and dashed from the room.

CHAPTER 11

A Good Heart

"Fritzi, how could you?" Karl cried out.

"Stop him!" Todd yelled.

"He'll ruin Christmas!" Jessica shouted.

They all ran out the door and down the hallway after Fritzi. Up ahead, Jessica could hear the *tingle-tingle-tingle* of the magic bell.

"He's going this way!" Amy said, waving them on.

As they skidded around the corner, they heard the bell again.

"Hurry!" Elizabeth said, running down another hall.

At the end of the hall, they saw a door swing shut. The Snoopers raced up to it. A sign on the door said, "Studio A. Quiet Please."

"He went into the Christmas special!" Amy said with a gasp.

She carefully opened the door, and they stole quietly into the studio. It was dark inside, and the Snoopers found themselves surrounded by tall cameras on stands, ladders, and pieces of video equipment. Several people stood with their backs to the Snoopers, watching the children on stage.

"How about you, Sally," the woman with the microphone asked one of the children. "What's your favorite thing about Christmas?"

Sally sat up straighter in her chair. "The best thing about Christmas is Santa Claus," she said. "I was in the hospital last year, and I was afraid he wouldn't be able to find me. But he did. I love him."

"Me, too," the boy next to her said. "He's wonderful. I asked Santa for a skateboard. If he brings me one, maybe I'll get well enough to ride it."

Jessica forgot all about finding Fritzi. She couldn't stop listening to the children talk about Santa Claus.

"What about you, Melissa?" the woman asked a girl in a wheelchair.

"Well, I love Santa, too," the girl answered. "But I especially love the elves. They work hard all year long to make presents for us. They must be so nice."

Next to Jessica, Karl sniffed and wiped his eyes.

"Psst," Lila whispered, nudging Jessica with her elbow. "There's Fritzi!"

Jessica peered into the darkness. Just a few feet away, Fritzi was standing in a shadow, staring at the stage.

"Come on," Todd said very softly. "Let's get him."

Step by step, the Snoopers crept up on Fritzi. When they got close enough, Elizabeth, Winston, and Amy grabbed him by the arms and shoulders.

Jessica stood in front of the elf. She opened her mouth to demand that he hand over the bell. But then she closed it again. Fritzi was crying.

"I'll give it back," he sobbed. "Nobody could ever take Santa's place, especially not me. Here, Karl. Take the bell back to Santa. It belongs to him."

Still crying, Fritzi put the magic jingle bell in Karl's hand. Karl gave his cousin a big hug.

80

"Hey!" someone whispered hoarsely. "What are you kids doing back here?"

"You're supposed to be sitting in the audience!" someone said, recognizing Amy.

Jessica backed up and tripped over a thick extension cord. "Whoa!" she yelled.

"Cut the tape!" a camera man said angrily. "Who's making all that racket?"

The overhead lights all came on. The Snoopers and the elves blinked hard and tried to see.

"Hey, it's that elf from the parade," a loud voice called out. "Don't let him leave. We're supposed to interview him next."

Before any of the Snoopers could take a step, a crowd of grown-ups surrounded them.

CHAPTER 12

Merry Christmas

A security guard put his hand on Karl's shoulder. "You're not going to escape from me. Everyone wants to know about what happened at the parade."

"Let go of him!" Jessica begged. "You don't understand."

Fritzi jumped up and down. "You big dummy!" he shouted to the guard. "There won't be a Christmas if you don't let Karl go!"

"Hey," the guard said angrily. "Nobody talks to me that way."

Elizabeth wanted to laugh. Fritzi was still rude, but she was sure he would never do anything nasty again.

"Please listen," Todd told the guard. "You can't keep Karl or Fritzi here. They have to get back to the North Pole."

All the adults laughed. "Sure, kid."

Todd looked embarrassed and angry.

Karl smiled up at the security guard. He was as friendly and cheerful as ever. "You know that rare baseball card you wanted when you were ten? Well, Santa's got a little surprise for you this year."

"Wh-what?" the security guard stammered in astonishment. "How did you—I mean, who told you—" In his confusion, he let go of Karl's shoulder.

"Good-bye, kids," Karl said. He pulled

Jessica down and kissed her on the cheek. "Thanks for everything."

Fritzi smiled. "So long everyone. And have a Merry Christmas."

Karl quickly clapped his hands over his head three times, grabbed Fritzi's hand, and rang the bell.

The two elves vanished.

"What happened?" a cameraman asked. "Where did they go?"

"Back to the North Pole," Lila answered. "We told you they were Santa's elves."

The grown-ups looked doubtful. "Now, kids," one of them said. "Why don't you just tell us what's going on? What kind of trick are you pulling?"

Elizabeth and Jessica looked at each other. No one would ever believe what had happened.

Only the Snoopers would know that Christmas had almost been ruined.

"They were real elves," Ellen explained patiently. "They came to find the magic bell."

"I'm sure *you* believe that, dear," the woman with the microphone said, patting her on the head. "But that simply can't be."

Through the open door, Elizabeth could see her father approaching. He had arrived to pick them up. When he saw all the commotion around the Snoopers, he hurried into the studio.

"What's all the fuss?" he asked. He turned to the security guard. "These are my daughters and their friends."

"Well, sir," the man said. "These kids here are involved in something very strange. See, these two other kids were pretending to be elves—"

"They *were* elves," Jessica said. "Honest, Dad. They were real elves."

Mr. Wakefield chuckled. "Honey, elves don't exist."

"They do, too," Elizabeth said. "They were real elves. They were real elves . . ."

Elizabeth opened her eyes. She was lying in her bed, in her bedroom. "They *were* real elves," she whispered to herself.

Puzzled, Elizabeth rolled over. Sitting on the night stand was Jessica's toy elf—Karl.

"Jessica?" she said, more confused than ever.

Jessica mumbled sleepily and pushed her covers back. She opened her eyes. "I had the most amazing dream," she said, sitting up. "I dreamed that my toy elf came to life and we had to help him find—"

"A magic bell?" Elizabeth's voice rose in surprise. "I had the same dream!"

Jessica and Elizabeth stared at each other. Something very strange was going on. Something like Christmas magic.

"We left that elf under the tree last night, didn't we?" Elizabeth said slowly, looking at the wooden elf.

Jessica nodded. "Look," she said. "His arm isn't cracked anymore.

They were both too puzzled to say anything else.

"Wake up, sleepyheads!" Mrs. Wakefield said cheerfully, opening the door. "It's time to make Christmas cookies. I need you girls to help me decorate a special cookie to leave out for Santa's snack tomorrow night."

Elizabeth looked at Jessica. Jessica looked at Elizabeth. Santa was coming tomorrow

night because the Snoopers, Karl, and Fritzi had found Donner's magic jingle bell and saved Christmas.

Hadn't they?